ZEKE PIPPIN

WILLIAM STEIG

SCHOLASTIC INC.

New York Toronto London Auckland Sydney

For Alicia, Ava Leigh, Courtney, Emma,
Graham, Jonas, Jonathan, Kate, Kevin, Lily,
Mariel, Peter, Timothy, and Will

ISBN 0-590-88019-5

12 11 10 9 8 7 6 5 4 3 2 1   7 8 9/9 0 1 2/0

Printed in the U.S.A.   08
First Scholastic printing, October 1997

Moseying down his street one morning, Zeke Pippin found a harmonica. He didn't exactly *find* it. It fell at his feet from a garbage wagon that happened to be rumbling by.

That piece of garbage changed his whole life.

Zeke took the harmonica home and thoroughly cleaned it with his tooth-brush, using his father's schnapps as a disinfectant. And then he spent countless hours, wherever he could find solitude, even out in the rain some-times, training his mouth to blow the sounds out and suck them in. He proved to be a natural musician.

Finally, one Sunday in June, when the family was lazing around the living room, Zeke whipped out his harmonica and started regaling them with the prelude to *La Traviata*. "Wow!" said his sister. "Bravo, Zekey!" his mother cried.

Even his father crowed, "Isn't that boy a Pippin."

But the next moment they were all fast asleep! And it was the same story at every single one of Zeke's would-be concerts. Somehow the Pippins went out like a light, no matter how merry the music.

Their rudeness (his father not only slept but snored) was like a slap in the face. "Is this bunch really my family, the ones who claim they love me?" Zeke asked. "How can I go on living under the same roof with such nincompoops?"

Zeke pretended to be indifferent to this insulting behavior, but one night he secretly packed two suitcases, the first with food, the second mostly with food. At the brink of dawn, with his harmonica in one pocket and all his cash in the other, he tiptoed down the stairs and left home.

Zeke lugged his bags down to his "private beach," where he had a raft hidden in the bushes. He dragged it out and made sure it was shipshape, then shoved and shimmied it into the river, loaded it with his stuff, and hopped aboard.

And there he was. As the red sun rose, the independent Zeke Pippin was drifting down the Hinkaholly River, face-to-face with the wide-open sky. Sometimes his raft turned this way, sometimes that way, and sometimes it twisted completely around.

After a while he snacked on a slew of bagels plastered with peanut butter. Later, when his mouth came unglued, he zeezled and zoozled on his harmonica.

Stuffed with bagels, Zeke nodded off. Nodding back on, he noticed he had company—an egret. He decided to treat his visitor to some good music. Guess what happened. The bird fell fast asleep. Just like his family!

Hmm. Zeke studied his instrument, and for the first time it struck him that it had no label. Was this some kind of weird magic harmonica that had fallen from the town garbage?

An excursion boat, churning up the river, presented the opportunity for an experiment. Zeke launched into a jolly folk tune, and as he pretty much expected, the passengers started clapping—then dozed off.

No two ways about it now. Zeke was the owner of a supernatural mouth organ.

Pondering this remarkable piece of garbage, he slid into dreamland. There he found his poor mother and father, and his poor brother and sister, all crying their hearts out, showering their clothes and the carpet with hot tears, asking how they could possibly go on without their oh-so-beloved Ezekiel. "If I don't see my angel again soon," his mother wailed, "I'll shoot myself!"

Zeke woke up crying too, reviling himself for his lack of faith in his family. He knew he must bring them surcease of their sorrow, as swiftly as possible, and clear up this painful misunderstanding. And since the raft wouldn't float upstream, he'd have to find his way home on foot.

As the sun was thinking of setting, Zeke was struggling to reach shore, pausing now and then to fortify himself with some licorice.

"Take it easy, pal, we'll help you," called the first of three dogs who came wading out.

"Thanks a million, guys," Zeke cried as the dogs tugged him in.

But once on solid ground, the Samaritans began researching his baggage.

"Hey, look at this," the leader chortled, "coconut mushmellow cookies!"

"Lay off," Zeke said. "It's *my* stuff!"

"Ha ha, it's *his* stuff," joked the one-eared foxhound.

"Yipes! A harmonica," yelped the dalmatian, yanking it from Zeke's pocket.

"Money!" the foxhound announced, digging into his other pocket.

"Have a heart, fellas," Zeke pleaded. "Give me my harmonica and let me go. *Please.* You can keep the rest—all of it."

"Listen, porky," the leader snarled, "you'd better shut your yap if you want to stay in one piece."

The dogs hustled Zeke to a run-down shack, where they tied his arms behind his back and began debating how to dispose of him.

"Let's drown him," the dalmatian suggested.

"How about baking him?" said the hound. "We could have baked ham, ham sandwiches, chitlins, pig's knuckles, et cetera."

"Nope, he's too darned fat," said the leader. "We'll just leave him here, nicely tied up."

"How about a goodbye song?" said the dalmatian. She pressed the harmonica to her lips, but all that came out was *FROO FRA FREE FRINK!*

"Put a lid on it!" barked the leader.

"I can show you what to do," Zeke offered, "if you untie me."

"We ain't untyin' nobody," said the leader.

"All right, don't untie me. Just hold it to my mouth."

The dalmatian obliged, Zeke commenced to play, and exactly as he'd planned, the villains conked out. As the dalmatian dropped to the floor, Zeke managed to hang on to the harmonica with his teeth.

He slipped past the criminals he'd so cleverly bamboozled, butted the door open, and started up the path by the river.

With the half-moon half helping, Zeke threaded his way through a confusion of trees and tangled vines. The world around him was still. Even the trees were asleep.

But then, out of that silence, came a frightful yowling...

Two nanoseconds later a death-dealing coyote had him pinned to the ground. Zeke was so scared he couldn't breathe. But when the coyote's claws pierced his flesh, he somehow squeezed out the opening bars of the only song that came to mind: "Show Me the Way to Go Home."

The coyote keeled over and yowled no more. Zeke played on a bit longer, to make double-sure the wretched carnivore was unconscious. Then he wriggled to his feet and continued homeward.

Bushed and bleary as he was, Zeke never figured out how he found his way. But at last he was there. Home. Where he belonged. He wiped his feet on the doormat, pressed the doorbell with his snout, and fainted.

His mother opened the door. "Pa-a-a!" she screamed. "Our boy is back! Do you hear me?"

"Zekey! Gazeek!" his father cried. "Welcome home!"

Zeke's father carried him to his bed, where he was covered with a blanket of kisses. Then they all spent the day waiting to hear his harrowing tale. (You already know it.)

Zeke was soon the darling of the town, more celebrated than even the mayor. Grateful parents smothered him with hugs for serenading their children to sleep. And patients in the Quayhogue Hospital unanimously preferred his music to sleeping pills.

For his next birthday, Zeke's parents gave him a regular harmonica, which he often played at the Grange Hall before an enraptured audience.

As for the garbage harmonica, he always kept it on his person. He would have felt naked without it.